MISHAWAKA-PENN PUBLIC LIBRARY

W9-AZY-500

pb

y   Modell, Frank   cop. 1
            Look out, it's April
Fools' Day

Reader-1

DISCARD

Mishawaka-Penn Public Library
Mishawaka, Indiana

LOOK OUT, IT'S APRIL FOOLS' DAY

FRANK MODELL

GREENWILLOW BOOKS, NEW YORK

MISHAWAKA - PENN PUBLIC LIBRARY
MISHAWAKA, INDIANA

For my cousin Florence

Copyright © 1985 by Frank Modell
All rights reserved. No part of this book
may be reproduced or utilized in any form
or by any means, electronic or mechanical,
including photocopying, recording or by
any information storage and retrieval
system, without permission in writing
from the Publisher, Greenwillow Books,
a division of William Morrow & Company, Inc.,
105 Madison Avenue, New York, N.Y. 10016.
Printed in the United States of America
First Edition

1 2 3 4 5 6 7 8 9 10

Library of Congress Cataloging in Publication Data
Modell, Frank.
Look out, it's April Fools' Day.
Summary: Marvin loves to play jokes on his
friend Milton, but on April Fools' Day,
Milton just won't be fooled.
[1. April Fools' Day—Fiction.
2. Jokes—Fiction.]   I. Title.
PZ7.M714Lo   1985   [E]   84-4138
ISBN 0-688-04016-0
ISBN 0-688-04017-9 (lib. bdg.)

#10557774

Marvin loved to play jokes on Milton.

Especially on April Fools' Day.

But this April Fools' Day
Milton couldn't be tricked.

"Look at that airplane," said Marvin.
"You can't fool me," said Milton.
"I know there's no airplane up there."

"You're no fun. April Fools' Day is supposed to be fun," said Marvin.

"That's because you tried to fool me
with the same dumb jokes last year,"
said Milton. "Remember?"

"If I think of some new ones,
  I bet I can fool you."
"I doubt it," said Milton.
"Your jokes are silly."

"No they're not,"
said Marvin.
"Besides jokes
are supposed
to be silly.
It's not a joke
if it's serious."

"Wow! Look at that."

"Really, Milton. Look! Two big green chickens."

"I'm not falling for that," said Milton.

"Oh boy! Spaceships," said Marvin.

"And a flying rabbit and the
biggest banana I ever saw."

"Look, Milton! Bows and arrows
and maybe Indians, too.
And there goes a big giant."

"Oh sure," said Milton.
"And a lady giant, too, I bet."

"That's right," said Marvin.
"And two little giants."

"That's silly. Who ever heard of little giants?"

"Look out," said Marvin.
"There's a big green snake right in back of you.
And a grizzly bear in back of the snake."

"Oh Marvin, why don't you give up?
You can't fool me," said Milton.

DAMAGE NOTED

"Hey, Milton, your shoelace is untied."
"Yours is too, Marvin."

"That's funny—I was only kidding."
"I was, too."
"April Fool, Marvin."
"April Fool, Milton."

MISHAWAKA - PENN PUBLIC LIBRARY
MISHAWAKA, INDIANA